by AFI SCRUGGS

pictures by DAVID DIAZ

THE BLUE SKY PRESS
An Imprint of Scholastic, Inc. • New York

THE BLUE SKY PRESS

Library of Congress catalog card number: 98-12857

ISBN 0-590-69327-1

10 9 8 7 6 5 4 3 2 1   0/0 01 02 03 04

Printed in Singapore   46

First printing, March 2000

To Sapriya and Shimeka, the jump-rope magicians

—A. S.

For Claudia, Rebekah, and Hannah

—D. D.

The rope started turning, and Shameka started jumping.
Her friends yelled out,
"Hey, Shameka, sing something!"

Shameka jumped so hard that her braids bounced about.
She thought for a minute, and then she called out:
"Hey, crew!"
"What?"
"Are you ready?"
"For what?"
"To jig!"
"Jig what?"
"Jig-a-low!"
"Let's go!"

"Jig-a-low, jig, jig-a-low, you sing it!"
"Jig-a-low! Jig-a-low!"

"Our hands are high, our feet are low,
and this is the way that we jig-a-low.

And-uh-one, and-uh-two,
and Shameka, who are you?"

"I'm the girl with the motion,
wave my hands like the ocean.
I can jump so high,
till I reach the sky."

"And-uh-one, and-uh-two,
and Shameka, who are you?"

"I'm the one who knows what she's gonna do.
I can jump one time, and then I'm through!"

Out, out, out!
Shameka jumped out.

She ran to her friends who were standing in a line.
They were bouncing in rhythm to the jump rope rhyme.
The rope was humming in the soft, warm air.
Jump rope music was everywhere!

Jump rope music in the sound of their feet,
skipping over rope and hitting concrete.

"Cinderella dressed in yellow
went upstairs to meet her fellow.
Made a mistake, and kissed a snake.
How many doctors did it take?
One, two, three . . ."

Shameka jumped up and turned around.

Bent down low and touched the ground.

Came up fast and started to laugh!
She saw diamonds in the grass!
She saw broken bottles shine
like rubies on a tomato vine.

Grass and flowers swayed in time.
Leaves clapped out the jump rope rhyme.

The jump rope beat soared on the breeze,
scattering magic through the trees.

Now, mean Miss Minnie was alone in her house.

Her head was in her hands, she was worrying on her couch.

When she heard the children laughing, she got real mad.

"Why should they be happy when I'm so sad?"

She stomped out the door and slammed it real hard.

"I'm gonna send those kids to their own backyards."

When the kids saw Miss Minnie, they began to run away.

They knew all the rude things she would say.

She fussed every time they jumped double Dutch.

She didn't like children, and she wanted them to hush.

But Shameka stood still.

She was having too much fun

with the music and the magic.

She wasn't gonna run.

She was gonna jump rope if she had to jump alone.

She was gonna jump rope. Nope, she wasn't going home.

Shameka took the rope that her friends left behind.
She started skipping fast to a brand-new rhyme.

"Hey, Miss Minnie,
can you come outside?
I got a new car.
Let's go for a ride.
We can put the top down.
We can blow the horn loud.
We can show the gold rims.
We can captivate the crowd."

Miss Minnie frowned hard. Who was this little girl?
She had never heard such talk! Her head began to whirl.

Quick as a breath the music touched her toes.
It circled 'round her knees and rose to her nose.
She tried to stand quiet 'cause she didn't want to care.
But the sadness left her eyes. She saw joy everywhere:

The diamonds in the grass,
the rubies on the vine,
the flowers in the pots
danced the jump rope rhyme.

Mean Miss Minnie jumped to her feet.
She sniffed the magic of the jump rope beat.
Her back straightened up and her fingers got popping,
and she leaped in the air with her mouth be-bopping:

"Shimmy, shimmy ko ko bop.
Shimmy, shimmy bop.
If you think you're bad as me,
watch me while I top your hop."

She twirled Shameka's rope till her legs topped the trees.
Shameka heard her singing as she floated past the leaves.

"I can jump so high,
I can reach the sky.
And I won't come back
till the Fourth of July.
I won't come back
till after Christmas Eve.
Good-bye, good-bye,
don't look for me!"

Shameka stretched her neck and looked into the sky.
She called to Miss Minnie as she saw her going by.

"Where will you go? Where will you go?"

"I'm going to heaven,
and I won't come down.
I'll be sitting on the moon
where I can't see the ground."

Shameka shouted out,
"Are you coming back this way?
Are you ever coming back?
Will you hear us when we play?"

"I'm not coming back,
but I'll hear every song.
I'm gonna leave you one.
You can sing it when I'm gone:
I'm flying past the land,
I'm flying past the sea.
And you have seen
the last of me!"

Shameka blinked once, and the rope was at her feet.
It was waiting for the music of the jump rope beat.

She ran through the neighborhood, rounding up her crew.
Once they got together, they all knew what to do.

The rope started turning, and Shameka started jumping.
Her crew cried out,
"Hey, Shameka! Sing something!"

Shameka jumped up, and she didn't hesitate.
She knew Miss Minnie could hardly wait
to hear how they would sing her rhyme,
the good-bye song she'd left behind.

"Pump the rope! Pump, pump the rope! You sing it!"

"Pump the rope! Pump, pump the rope!"

"I'm gonna jump real hard."
"Go girl!"

"I'm gonna jump real high."
"You go!"

"Gonna jump so high, I'll touch the sky
like fireworks on the Fourth of July.
Gonna fly to the moon and when I come home,
gonna jump one time, and then I'm gone!"
"Go girl!"

"Gonna fly across the land."
"You go!"

"Gonna fly across the sea."
"Go girl!"

"And you have seen the last of me!"

Out, out, out!

Shameka
jumped
out!

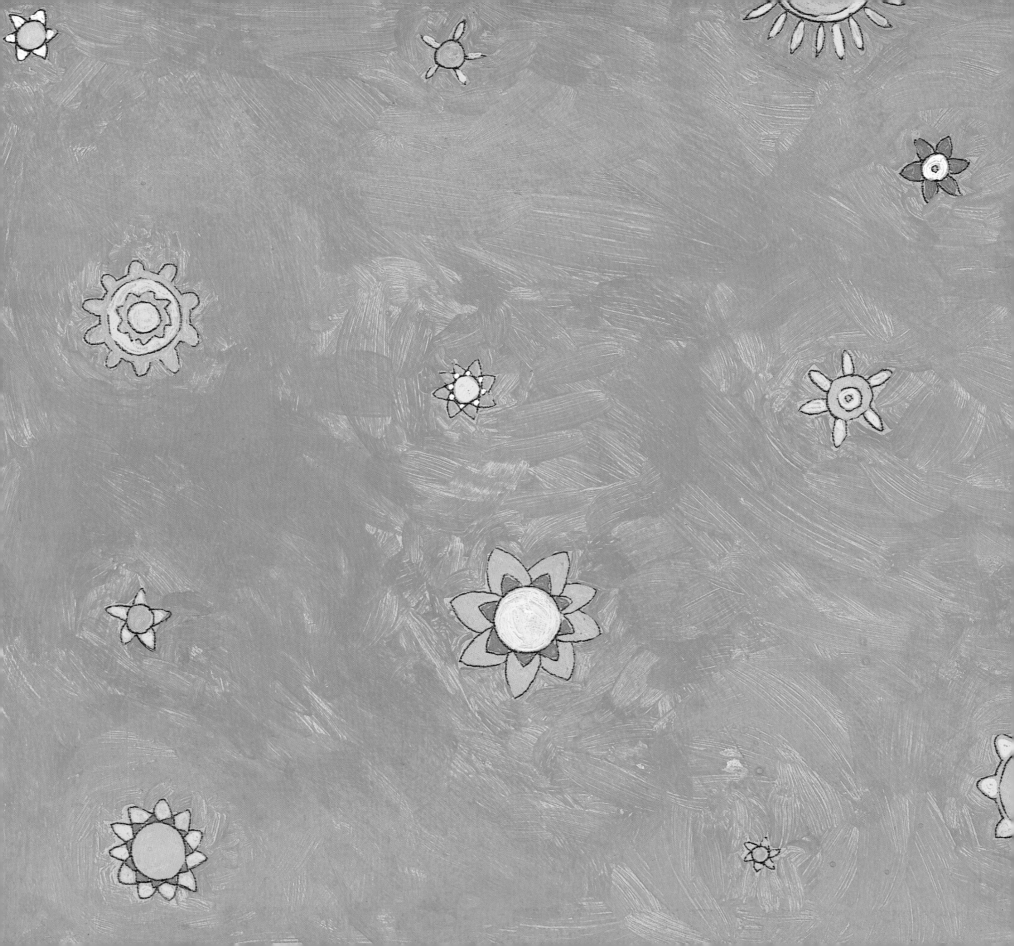